Shared with Santa

A Spicy Holiday Fantasy

Lacey Cross

Paperback ISBN: 978-1-960162-22-9

CONTENTS

To those who believe in holiday magic and sharing the joy.

CHAPTER 1

"Mom?"

I stop daydreaming and glance over at my beautiful 25-year-old daughter staring at me from across the kitchen table as we decorate Christmas cookies.

"Hmm?"

The holiday season always makes me spacey. I spend a lot of time reminiscing about past holidays. I've had a full life, but Christmas is always my favorite time of the year.

"I was asking you if anyone in your family had their hair go white at my age."

She points at the top of her head, as if I haven't noticed the snow white hair growing in.

"I mean, there has to be a reason for this...right?"

I inwardly smile and debate whether to tell her genetics doesn't always have rhyme or reason...or something else. The expectant look on her face tells me she doesn't want to hear the scientific explanation.

Setting my frosting-covered knife down on my plate, I fold my hands in my lap. "It's time to tell you a story."

She arches her eyebrow, but says nothing.

"'Twas the night before Christmas, when all through the house, not a creature was stirring...except my stomach because I was starving."

She snorts, and I mentally drift as I daydream. So much of this story is not safe for her ears.

I hate that my birthday falls on Christmas. Whenever I complain about it to my mom, she jokes and reminds me she spent Christmas in the hospital birthing my ungrateful ass. She's not wrong, but she's the one who wanted me. Am I supposed to thank her for that?

I love my parents, so I'm excited to be home for a couple of weeks for Christmas break, even if that means leaving my boyfriend, Michael, behind. I'm a freshman at college, and since it's now after midnight, I'm officially 19. My parents went to bed a couple of hours ago, and I pretended I was tired as well. It was just an excuse to be alone and not stay up talking to my little sister.

Plus, I had plans.

I met Michael during new-student orientation, and we've been inseparable for the last couple of months. We're not officially a couple, because we aren't ready to commit to something our freshman year, but we recently decided it was time to take our relationship to the next level when I get back from winter break. I'm finally going to have sex.

I hope it feels as good as all my friends claim.

I settle in on my bed as my body tingles at the thought of our upcoming sexy plans. Moving my hand between my legs, I rub myself through my pajama bottoms. Michael treats me so damn good, and it's been difficult to wait as long as we have. We almost went all the way several times while making out, but we both want our first time together to be special and not in the backseat of his car.

I imagine his deep brown eyes boring into mine. It's his hand rubbing my pussy as a damp patch forms on the fabric. Why am I even wearing these? I don't need them.

I shimmy out of my pajamas and underwear, leaving my long sleep shirt on. Spreading my legs, I brush my fingers over my slick folds and moan when I press a finger inside my pussy to gather moisture. Shit, I'm so wet. I wish Michael were here with me.

I've had nothing bigger than a couple of fingers inside me. The condom-covered cucumber I once tried to fuck myself with doesn't count — I couldn't get it in. My slick fingers glide over my clit, and I flex my hips against my hand as pleasure swirls from my core.

What is it going to feel like to have a cock pressing inside me for the first time? I close my eyes and picture Michael above me with his cock ready for that first glorious thrust. My body tenses, and I'm already close to an orgasm as I think about the future. I can't wait.

Right before Michael takes that first plunge, his body and face morph into one of a sexy silver fox with a white beard. He's naked, but I know it's Santa. His eyes twinkle, and I imagine him calling me "baby girl."

Oh fuck, that's hot.

I keep swirling my fingers around my clit as the bliss mounts. I've never masturbated to a fictional character before, but I'm getting even more worked up as I imagine it's Santa sliding his thick cock inside me. My toes curl from the ecstasy as I almost come.

Would Santa be gentle and loving? Or rough and commanding? He could probably fuck me for hours. I already know Michael is a soft lover, but somehow Santa knows what I want and is willing to do all the filthy things I can never admit to Michael.

I'm so horny I don't care that I'm fantasizing about another man. Right now, all I need is a big, hard imaginary cock to make me come. I rock my hips faster and moan. I'm just about to tip over the edge when a loud grumble from my stomach distracts me.

Ugh, what the fuck? Now is NOT the time for my stomach to remind me that dinner was hours ago. I intended to have a snack and then I forgot in my haste to be alone.

I slow down my finger fucking and grumble. Once the thought of food enters my mind, I need to eat something or I'll never come. Shit, this sucks.

Dragging myself off the bed, I wipe my fingers on my nightshirt but don't put on panties or my pajama pants. My nightshirt covers everything necessary unless I bend over. I'm only grabbing something quick from the kitchen, and I'll bring it back upstairs to eat. As quietly as possible, I creep down the carpeted hall. I don't want to alert my sister that I'm awake.

I snag a banana and a muffin from the kitchen, and I'm eying the banana speculatively as I wander into the living room to give one last admiring glance to the Christmas tree full of gifts. Tonight is the last night to see it in all its glory for the season.

Munching on the muffin, I'm startled by a clank from the chimney. What the hell? I set the muffin and the banana on an end table and move closer to the fireplace. It sounds like something is up there.

I crouch in front of it, intending to look up the chimney, when a pair of black boots and red legs dangle in front of me. I fall backwards silently, too shocked to scream, land on my back with my legs splayed. As I lean up on my elbows, Santa — no, some dude who looks like the Santa of my dreams — climbs out of the fireplace.

He's massive, with a rounded belly and dressed like Santa would be. A red sack is slung over his shoulder, presumably full of gifts. He's also oddly clean for just having come down the dirty chimney.

He stands up to his full height and stares down at me. "Well, hello there. I was expecting cookies and milk, but this is an even better surprise."

What?

I look at myself and realize my nightshirt is at my waist and I'm lying with my knees bent. My wet pussy is on full display. Oh, fuck. My eyes fly to Santa's, and I open my mouth to tell him he can forget his pervy plans, but his blue eyes twinkle from the multicolor lights on the tree and I'm mesmerized. My entire body buzzes alive, and my nipples pucker into hard pebbles. Wetness leaks from my slutty cunt, and I clench my muscles from a jolt of pleasure.

Okay, I must have fallen asleep before coming downstairs for food. None of this is real. It takes my brain all of two seconds to consider everything...hell, this might be the best sex dream I've ever had.

A smile softens my face, and I lift one hand, curling my finger in a come-hither motion. "Then come here, big boy, and get your gift."

He drops the red sack on the floor and moves to unbuckle his belt. "Oh yeah, baby girl. Santa is going to give you the best Christmas present ever."

This is an amazing dream. Santa better fuck me hard. I pull my nightshirt up, bunching it above my tits, and expose the firm globes to him. I play with a nipple, and he keeps his eyes trained on my hand as he undresses. As his clothes fall to the floor, I'm amazed to realize the belly was a padded suit. Once he's naked, Santa is muscular and a gorgeous silver fox. Oh, hell yeah.

The lust in his eyes is unmistakable, as is the hardness of his cock once he finally frees it. Jesus, that thing is huge. Well, of course it is. This is my dream, after all.

He kneels between my legs and rubs his hands along my wet folds. "Someone is all wet for Santa."

I moan from the pleasure and arch my back, opening my thighs wider. "Yes, Daddy."

I'm not sure why I called him 'Daddy,' but it felt right, and he hums in approval at the word. As he dips a finger into my soaked pussy, I gasp at the invasion. God, his one finger is so damn thick. How big is his cock? I try to get a peek at his package, but he distracts me when he moves his juice-coated finger to his mouth and sucks on it.

"You taste delicious. Were you touching yourself before I got here?"

I nod and blush.

"Someone has been a very naughty girl."

Is that not allowed? It's not like I knew Santa was coming to visit. Wait, should I tell him I'm a virgin?

Shit, if I do, will he be gentle? I don't want that. But I also don't want too much pain.

I war with myself for a moment, but when he moves the head of his cock and presses it against my opening, I decide I better tell him.

I flutter my eyes at him and use my cutest voice. "Santa, I should warn you. I've never been with a man before."

He pauses. "Never?"

Biting my lower lip, I shake my head. "Never, but I want you to be my first."

My first time fucking Santa in my dreams, that is.

When he swirls his finger around my clit and doesn't make a move to fuck me again, the pings of bliss make me desperate. "Please, Daddy, will you fuck me?"

He scoots forward and presses his cock to my dripping slit. "That's what I'm here for, baby girl. I just had to wrap my head around a pretty little thing like you being a virgin."

Since this is only a dream, my sluttiest side comes out.

I arch my hips toward him and whimper, "Daddy, please fuck me already. I'm so ready for you to fill me up with that thick, hard cock of yours."

He growls and slides just the tip inside me. Mmmm. God, I can't believe this is happening, even if it's just a dream.

A brief second of pressure is all the warning I get before he slams into me, tunneling past any resistance. Pain lances through me and I cry out from the sudden invasion. I'm stretched and filled more than I expected. I don't know how big Michael's cock is comparatively, but Santa feels enormous.

He sinks the last few inches into me and waits while I adjust to his size. Now that he's inside me, there's surprisingly little pain beyond that initial shock. I flex my hips and fiery sparks of pleasure shoot from my pussy. Heat infuses my face and my lips fall open as I gasp from the sensation.

There's no way I should feel this good in a dream.

"It's time for Santa to fuck you, baby girl. I've got a powerful need to fill your pretty pussy."

God, I've really got a filthy mind...but this is fabulous.

Santa grips my hips and starts pumping in and out. Each thrust hits a different spot inside me, and the sensations are overwhelming. I whimper and roll my hips, giving him a better angle. I gaze down between us, watching his thick shaft, glistening with my juices, thrust into me. Too bad the living room doesn't have a mirror. I bet this would look awesome.

His hard, rough strokes rock my body. All I can do is quiver and moan as he jackhammers into me.

I want more.

"Harder, Daddy. Harder!"

Oh yeah, I'm a dirty girl. My filthy words don't shock me anymore.

He grabs my breasts and squeezes them as he pounds into me. The room spins as the delight builds. I'm so damn close to coming. Wiggling my hips, I try to tempt him to pound even deeper. The pleasure is almost painful, but I'm loving it. I need to come, but I also don't want this dream to end.

Moving my arms above my head, I arch my back and marvel at how freeing and raunchy this is. I didn't even know I wanted this, and suddenly it's the top fantasy of all time.

His voice is thickened with desire when he speaks. "Is my baby girl ready to be bred by Santa?"

"Ohhhh," I moan.

Him saying he's going to breed me is extra filthy. I'm not on birth control, but it doesn't matter. Since I'm making this all up, I know he's going to have ropes and ropes of thick cum that will gush out of me when he's done with me.

"Beg," he demands. "Beg for me to breed you."

He's fucking me vigorously, and I'm being knocked around like a rag doll.

All I can do is gasp out, "Oh god, breed me, Daddy. Fill me until I'm dripping. I need your cum so bad. Please? Oh god, please?"

He growls. "I'll give you exactly what you want, baby girl. I'm going to fill you so full of my seed, you're going to beg me to breed you again and again."

Holy shit.

I've never heard anything more erotic in my life. As he continues to pound into me, my muscles tighten and I start to twitch.

I'm so far gone, I can't talk.

He continues, thrusting sharply between each word. "My...perfect...little...breeding...toy. Now come for me."

I cry out as I erupt. Blissful, blistering pleasure overwhelms me. My mind splinters, and then there is no thinking. I'm moaning and jerking uncontrollably while he drives in to me, seeking his own release. I'm just a vessel awaiting his seed.

He bucks and moans until he stiffens and explodes with a roar of satisfaction. The hot spray of his seed floods into me and coats my cave walls. The aftershocks of my orgasm cause me to clamp down on his shaft, milking him for every drop until he slows down and pulls out.

He moves from between my legs, and I collapse. My brain is a puddle of mush, but I have enough awareness to feel his cum sliding out of me. Thank god this is a dream so there won't be any clean up.

His voice is low and gruff. "I might have to come visit you every year. You're a delightful treat."

I give a soft laugh and a "mmm" as he stands up and retrieves his Santa outfit. I'm floating in a daze, and before I know it, he's standing over me, fully dressed.

"Baby girl, rest a few minutes, but then you need to clean up and go to bed. Don't fall asleep down here." He gestures towards the banana and half-eaten muffin. "And eat your snack and drink. Stay healthy so I can visit you again next year."

I murmur, "Yes, Daddy," and close my eyes and drift. It's not long before the stillness of the room makes me open my eyes, and I can see I'm alone.

Best Christmas Ever!

CHAPTER 2

Tonight is Christmas Eve — my second Christmas as a married woman — and my husband, Michael, and I already have our own tradition. We put our 15-month-old daughter to bed an hour ago, and I'm in a silky red nightie that ends right below my ass. The only thing Michael is wearing is flannel pajama pants as he sits on the recliner by the Christmas tree and waits for me.

The twinkling lights on the tree are the only thing illuminating the darkened room, casting shadows against the wall as I walk in and pause in front of him. "Do you like the nightie?"

He doesn't answer, and his focus shifts to my breasts. Even in the dim light, I see his pupils dilate as he imagines what's underneath my top. With his dark, trimmed beard, chestnut hair, and brown eyes, he's a beautiful man who stole my breath the moment I met him. We didn't plan to get married this young, but when I got pregnant right after Christmas two years ago, everything changed. I've never regretted it for a moment, and our beautiful daughter is a testament to this being the perfect life for me.

I straddle him and kiss him deeply, purring, "A smart husband would tell me I'm gorgeous if he wants a chance to see what's underneath it."

When he only kisses me harder, I wonder how much teasing I'll get away with. Usually, I tempt him until he loses control and fucks me roughly on the couch. I shiver as I remember the last time he did, but we have a busy life so it's hard to carve out time for ourselves, and it doesn't happen that often. Tonight is a treat.

I can feel his hardness, and I fit him perfectly against my pussy and grind against him. He moves his hands to my ass and slides them under the nightie, groaning when he realizes I'm not wearing any panties.

I rock against him, the pleasure building, as he nips at my neck and sends tendrils of delight down my spine. His voice is lust-tinged as he whispers, "Tell me the story again."

And there it is...our tradition.

I moan and close my eyes, rolling my hips and daydreaming about that Christmas Eve two years ago.

"I was visiting my parents..."

He pushes my nightie up past my breasts, and, before sucking on a nipple, he growls, "Skip ahead to the good part."

As his warm tongue twirls around my nipple, I moan, "You mean when Santa shoved his huge cock into me and took my virginity?"

Michael sucks on the other tit, and I grind against him, almost lost in the pleasure. "Or do you mean when Santa filled me with ropes of thick, sticky cum and bred me?"

My husband swears softly under his breath and grasps my hips, forcing me to stop moving. I can tell he almost just lost it and came. To torture him a little, I shimmy my hips and he swears again. "Damnit, Shanna, you're going to make me come before it's time."

I kiss him softly to hide my smile. Doesn't he realize that's the point?

Right before I start moving my hips again, the grandfather clock we got as a wedding gift chimes the time, letting us know it's officially Christmas.

"Merry Christmas, Michael," I whisper, knowing it's almost time for gifts.

He smiles. "Happy birthday, babe."

My stomach buzzes with anticipation. It's my birthday!

Growing up, I hated having my birthday today, but the last two years, I've grown to love it. Good things happen when your birthday is on Christmas.

The clank from the chimney doesn't scare me. Instead, anticipation zings through my body as both Michael and I watch a pair of black boots and red legs emerge from our chimney. It's Santa!

When he steps out, he's clean with no sign of soot. The room fills with excitement and energy. It's magical. I can feel Michael's cock pulsing between us, and my nipples harden into diamonds as I imagine what's about to happen.

As Santa tosses the red sack to the floor, his eyes scan down my body. His eyes twinkle as he takes in the sight of me straddling Michael. "Getting our naughty girl warmed up for me, I see."

I giggle, and say, "Yes, Daddy," to Santa, and my husband's cock throbs against my pussy again. Yeah, Michael likes this part.

Santa removes his suit with the padded belly, revealing the muscular silver fox of my dreams beneath. Once he's naked, his magnificent, thick cock juts straight out, and the shadows of the room with the twinkling lights gives this a surreal feel. This is the third visit from Santa, and each time, it feels like a dream.

And now for the part that I like.

I climb off Michael and sink to my knees, crawling in front of Santa before peeling off my nightie and tossing it aside. I'm an exhibitionist at heart, and I love showing off my trim body to my husband, and now Santa.

"Santa, is there a place for me on the Naughty list?"

He laughs. "There's always room for one more." He turns his focus to Michael. "Are you ready to watch me breed your wife's sweet little pussy?"

Michael's eyes lock with mine as he answers. "Yes."

Butterflies swirl in my stomach as Santa's jolly laugh rings out. "Right-o, then let's get a look at that pussy, baby girl. I've got a need for you again. It's been a long year."

I'm a slut, and I can't help it. I lie back on the carpet in front of him, spreading my legs and putting my feet flat on the floor...very much like the position I was in when he first found me two years ago and took my virginity.

Wetness leaks from my pussy as Santa kneels between my legs and runs his fingers up and down my pussy lips. "Now that's what I'm talking about."

I whimper as he plays with my wet folds. "Please, Daddy, fuck me."

He lifts his fingers to his nose and sniffs, moaning, "It's time for Christmas to come."

The head of his cock presses against my opening, and with one thrust, he plunges his fat cock into my hot, welcoming entrance. My body jerks, and a deep moan erupts from me as he stretches me out. Am I ever going to get used to the size of his massive cock? It seems bigger every time I see it.

With no desire to resist his invasion, my muscles relax and allow him to bury himself deep inside me. As he rocks his pelvis, the pleasure begins to build, and I feel as if

I'm floating on a cloud. There's something magical about this moment every time it happens. I swear the room is brighter, with more dancing lights from the tree and stars shining more brightly through the windows.

Santa is an all-consuming presence, and I cling to his shoulders as he thrusts into me, his voice a husky murmur. "Naughty girl, letting Santa's cock fill you while your husband watches."

Oh shit, that's so damn good. I'm a slut for dirty talk, and Santa knows exactly what to say to make my head spin.

Santa continues with the dirty talk. "Just a little fucktoy that likes being used and bred by Santa. You're desperate for it, aren't you?"

Oh god, that's so good. I moan, "Yes," as pings of bliss explode in my mind.

He slams me against the carpet with his savage fucking, and I glance over at Michael to make sure he's enjoying the show. Michael's cock is out, and he's pumping it furiously. Watching my husband pleasure himself while Santa fucks me intensifies my lust even further.

Santa's cock continues to slam against a sweet spot deep inside me, and my cries of passion echo through the room.

Santa's animalistic grunt of pleasure drowns out my cry. This is so intense, yet so needed, and I wouldn't change a thing about my life right now.

Our bodies move in perfect unison, a wild dance that drives us towards our ultimate bliss. My entire body is ablaze, and my toes curl as the pleasure builds in layers. I'm almost beyond thinking.

This is the third time I've been with Santa, but tonight is different from last year. As his thick shaft impales me, my inner muscles tighten in anticipation of the gift he's about to release. Just like two Christmases ago, when he visited to give me his seed, I'm certain that I'll have another precious gift inside me after tonight.

The thought of Santa breeding me pushes me over the edge. I scream out in pure, joyous release, and wave after wave of exquisite heat surges through my body. As my euphoria fades, Santa speeds up his thrusts and roars as he unleashes his load, coating my insides with his thick cum. He spasms and thrusts harder, emptying every last drop.

A groan from Michael makes me turn my head and watch him release the last of his cum on his stomach and hand as he drains his balls. Holy hell, watching him come pushes me to the brink again, and another mini-orgasm rockets through me while Santa continues to plow into me.

When Santa senses I've come down from my second orgasm, he buries himself one final time before freezing and letting out a contented sigh. Our labored breaths mix, and he kisses me gently, a stark contrast to the rough fucking he just gave me. When he breaks off the kiss, we're both laughing, our eyes hazy with after-sex bliss as he withdraws from me.

Once he's back on his knees between my legs, I find myself smiling up at him with happiness. He reaches out a hand to caress my cheek and gazes deep into my eyes. "You're welcome, my ho, ho, ho, and Merry Christmas to both of you. Thanks for inviting me back for a repeat performance."

Sitting up, I hug him, pressing my bare chest against his, and whisper in his ear, "Same time next year?"

Santa chuckles. "Baby girl, you can count on it."

Leaning back, I watch Santa get dressed again, the costume turning him into the round bellied Santa that everyone imagines.

When he picks up his bag, he gives me a gentle smile before turning to Michael. "Thank you for sharing your wife. She's always a delight."

Without waiting for a response, Santa heads towards the chimney and crawls back up into the fireplace. A few moments later, we hear his sleigh take off, and the entire house shakes and settles as the noise fades into silence.

It's over as quickly as it started.

Santa appears and disappears without a trace, making the whole experience feel like a dream. An incredible, amazing, fantastical dream that leaves me sated.

After we clean up, my husband holds me close in bed, kissing me and showing me that he still loves me. Closing my eyes, I snuggle in against him. This is heaven. I get my wonderful husband, and once a year, I get to be Santa's little fucktoy.

I couldn't wish for a better life.

CHAPTER 3

The kids are finally asleep, and I can hardly contain my excitement. It's Christmas Eve (and my birthday) again, a whole year since Santa's last visit, and the anticipation is killing me. I'm wearing a sheer green babydoll that barely covers my ass, and Michael's eyes haven't left my body since I slipped it on.

"You look incredible," he murmurs, pulling me onto his lap as he sits in the armchair by the twinkling Christmas tree. This seems to be the Christmas tradition, and I shiver at his touch as his hands roam over my thighs.

"Mmm, thank you," I purr, grinding against him. I can feel his hardness through his thin pajama pants, and it takes all my willpower not to impale myself on him right then and there. But we have to wait. Santa will be here soon.

Michael's lips find my neck, and I tilt my head to give him better access. "God, Shanna, you drive me crazy," he whispers against my skin. His beard tickles me, and I giggle softly.

He responds by sucking harder on my pulse point, and I have to bite my lip to keep from moaning. My nipples harden against the thin fabric of my lingerie, and Michael's hands move up to cup my breasts.

"Maybe we should start without him," Michael suggests, his voice husky with desire.

I shake my head, even as my body screams for more. "You know the rules, babe. We wait for Santa."

He groans in frustration, but I can see the excitement in his eyes. This has become our favorite tradition, and the anticipation is half the fun.

I lean in close, my lips brushing his ear. "Just think about how good it'll feel when he finally arrives. When you get to watch him fuck me senseless."

Michael's cock twitches against me, and I smirk. I love teasing him like this.

"Tell me what you want to see," I whisper, rolling my hips slowly.

He swallows hard. "I want to watch as he stretches you open with that massive cock of his."

My pussy clenches at the thought, and I feel a fresh wave of wetness between my thighs. "Mmm, and then what?"

"Then I want to see him pound you until you're scream-ing. Until you're begging for his cum."

God, my husband's filthy side is one of the best things about him. He's just as dirty-minded as I am. I'm about to respond when we hear a faint noise from the chimney. My heart races, and Michael and I lock eyes. This is it. It's time for Santa to come down our chimney.

"Merry Christmas, babe," I whisper, giving him one last deep kiss before climbing off his lap.

I stand in front of the fireplace, barely containing my excitement. It seems like ages since I've seen Santa. The rustling sounds from the chimney grow louder, and I peek at Michael. He's still in the armchair, and his eyes mirror my lust.

Finally, a pair of shiny black boots appear, followed by red-clad legs. I hold my breath as Santa squeezes out of the fireplace, looking as magnificent as ever. His blue eyes twinkle as they land on me, and a slow smile spreads across his face.

"Ho ho ho," he chuckles, his voice deep and rich. "What do we have here? A very naughty girl, it seems."

I bite my lip, playing coy. "Have I been bad this year, Santa?"

He steps closer, towering over me. I can smell his masculine scent, a mix of pine and cinnamon that makes my head spin. "Oh yes, very bad indeed. But that's just how I like you."

Santa's hand cups my cheek, and I lean into his touch. "Happy birthday, baby girl," he murmurs. "Are you ready for your present?"

I nod eagerly, already trembling with need. "Yes, Daddy. Please."

He grins wickedly, then turns to acknowledge Michael. "And you, young man? Are you ready to watch me unwrap my gift?"

Michael's voice is hoarse with desire when he responds. "Yes, Santa."

Santa's laugh booms through the room as he begins to undress. I watch, mesmerized, as he reveals his muscular body. When his massive cock springs free, I lick my lips and imagine what he tastes like.

"Now then," Santa growls, pulling me flush against him. "Let's see how naughty you can really be."

As his mouth crashes onto mine, I melt against him, ready for whatever delicious presents he has in store for me this Christmas. His lips devour mine as his hands roam over my body, igniting a wildfire of desire that threatens to consume me whole.

He breaks the kiss, his eyes blazing with a hunger. "Time to unwrap my gift, my filthy little present," he growls as he lifts me onto the couch with an ease that belies his massive frame.

I lie back, my heart racing in anticipation, and lift my legs to help Santa pull off my panties. He tosses them across the room to Michael, and Michael instinctually grabs them. Yeah...my husband is holding my wet panties. This is naughty.

I spread my legs for Santa, and his gaze lingers on my wet pussy. His fingers, thick and sure, trace the outline of my folds, and I shudder at the touch. "So ready for me, baby girl," he whispers, and his gruff tone makes my clit throb with need. "Your pussy's calling my name, and I'm more than happy to answer."

He kneels between my legs, and with one swift, merciless motion, he plunges his cock into me. The sudden invasion makes me gasp, and my body arches off the couch in a futile attempt to escape the overwhelming pleasure. I don't really want to escape. I want more of this glorious sensation, and I moan, "Oh, god, yes!"

Santa doesn't waste time as he pounds into me relentlessly. Each thrust is a branding iron that sears my soul and claims me as his fucktoy.

"You're a slut for my cock, aren't you?" he growls, his voice a challenging slap that my body responds to with a surge of wetness, welcoming him deeper. "Admit it, baby girl. Tell me how much you crave this."

As I'm ravished by the sheer intensity of Santa's thrusts, I steal a glance at my husband, knowing he's watching with rapt attention. The thought of his eyes on me, witnessing my transformation into a super slut, only heightens my arousal. I recall how he loves it when I let go, embracing my filthiest side for Santa alone. This knowledge sparks a dirty thrill within me, fueling my confession.

"Yes, I'm a slut for you, Santa. Only for you. I crave your cock, need it, can't live without it fucking me into oblivion." The words tumble out in a rush of shame and multiplying desire. I can almost sense my husband's silent encouragement, his pleasure in my debauchery.

Santa's response is immediate, his claim on me as possessive as his thrusts. "You're mine, then," he declares, his movements becoming shorter, more intense, as if driven to stake his very soul's claim on me. "Forever mine, my little fucktoy. I'm going to visit every Christmas and pound this pussy into submission while you beg for my cum."

Oh god, and I will. I know I will.

The bliss builds as Santa jackhammers into me and continues his dirty talk. "And your husband loves it. He loves how much of a slut you are for my thick cock. Look at him — look at how much he wants you to be my fucktoy every year."

The room spins as I glance at my wonderful husband. There's a wild look in his eyes as he focuses on the sight of

Santa plowing into me. His cock is out and he's stroking it with my panties. The sight makes me shiver in delight. Yep, that's my filthy man.

Santa chuckles. "That's right. He wants me to split you open every year and make you scream. He loves fucking you after I've blown my load deep inside you."

Fuuuuck, it's true. Every time Santa leaves, Michael loves to play with my pussy, and it always ends with Michael fucking Santa's cum back up inside me.

Santa's voice is harsh. "Ask me..."

I open my mouth, ready to ask for whatever he demands, but then I realize Santa is talking to Michael.

"Ask me to breed your wife. Say you want to see her take all my cum like a good girl."

Holy fuck, is Michael going to say it?

Michael's voice, though slightly hesitant, rings out clear in the sexually charged atmosphere. "Santa, I...I want to see her take all your cum like a good girl. Breed my wife, please."

I hold my breath as Santa's face splits into a wide, devilish grin. "Ah, excellent choice, young man. You want to watch me fill your wife to the brim, don't you?" He pauses, his gaze never leaving my flushed face. "Very well, I shall give you both exactly what you desire."

With renewed vigor, Santa pounds into me, his thrusts shorter and more intense. My cries of pleasure mingle with Michael's groans as he strokes himself, creating a sensual symphony that fills the room.

As the moment of climax approaches, Santa's voice rises through my haze of lust. "Here it comes, baby girl! Get ready to be filled with my Christmas gift!"

My body arches, my muscles tensing in anticipation as I scream, "Oh, god, yes! Fill me, Daddy!"

As Santa unleashes a torrent of cum deep within me, my body convulses, trapped in a maelstrom of ecstasy. I glance at Michael, and his expression of desire and wonder is branded on my brain as my orgasm crashes over me, leaving me gasping for air.

As I come down from my high, Santa's rhythm slows, and he pulls out, his cock glistening with my juices. "Now, baby girl, it's time for your real present," he says, his eyes sparkling with mischief.

I'm practically boneless from pleasure, and he pulls me off the couch to the floor. I'm on my stomach, and he yanks my hips up and forces me to my knees. I struggle to get into position, prepared to put my face to the carpet and let him do whatever he wants, but Santa has other plans.

"Get over here and fuck your wife. I've got a hankering for that filthy mouth of hers."

Oooh, I get both of them? I suddenly have more energy and I'm able to get up on my hands while Santa positions himself in front of me.

Michael doesn't waste any time as he moves behind my ass. "Yes, let's give her the ultimate Christmas gift."

Santa's cock — still somehow magically hard — bobs near my mouth as Michael grasps my hips. I feel the tip of his cock at my pussy a moment before he slides into me. He groans as he feels the combined wetness of my juices and Santa's cum.

As Michael starts to thrust into me, Santa's cock brushes against my lips. I open wide, taking him in, the salty taste of him mixed with my own essence explodes on my tongue. We rock together, each plunge from my husband forces Santa's cock deeper into my throat. I'm determined to be the best fucktoy for Santa, and I moan loudly as I enthusiastically suck on his cock.

When Michael whacks against me particularly hard, I squeal in delight and gurgle around Santa's shaft. God, I love it when Michael gets a little rough with me. It always means he's so far gone he's out of control.

My obvious enjoyment encourages Michael, and he picks up the tempo. The room fills with the sounds of our combined pleasure as Santa's cock fills my mouth, muffling my moans as Michael's thrusts become more urgent. I can feel his fingers digging into my hips, his body slapping against mine with a primal rhythm. The taste of Santa's cum mixed with my own juices is intoxicating, and I find myself lost in a haze of pleasure and filth.

Santa's hands are on my head, guiding my movements, his fingers tangled in my hair. I look up at him, my eyes watering as I take him deeper into my throat. He smiles down at me, his eyes filled with lust and something else — something almost tender.

"Fuck, yes, baby girl," he groans, his voice hoarse with pleasure. "You're taking my cock so well. You're such a good little slut for Santa."

His words send a surge of heat through me, and I feel my pussy clench around Michael's cock. Michael lets out a low groan, and when his thrusts become short and quick, I can tell he's ready to come. Santa's cock swells in my mouth, and I know he's close too. I want to taste him, to swallow every last drop of his cum. I want to be his filthy little present, his good little slut.

I suck harder, my cheeks hollowing out as I take him deeper. Santa's hands tighten in my hair, his body tensing as he lets out a low growl. His cock pulses in my mouth, and then he's coming, his hot cum filling my throat. I swallow greedily, my body shuddering with pleasure as I drink him down.

Behind me, Michael lets out a final groan, his body slamming into mine one last time before he stills. I can feel his cock pulsing inside me, his cum filling me, mixing with Santa's, and it's like a match to gasoline. My body ignites, every nerve ending exploding with pleasure. I scream around Santa's still-buried shaft as my orgasm tears through me. My pussy clamps down on Michael's cock, walls fluttering and milking his cock for every last drop. Waves of ecstasy radiate from my core, my body convulsing as if possessed. My vision goes white, and for a moment,

I'm lost, completely consumed by the intensity. I never want this feeling to end.

I'm not sure how much time passes, but my head spins as I come down from my high. My body shakes with after-shocks, and my heart is pounding. It wasn't just an orgasm; it was a fucking revelation. I was made to take Michael's and Santa's cocks. I want this every year for the rest of my life.

We stay like that for a moment, our bodies connected, our breaths ragged. Then Santa pulls out of my mouth, a satisfied smile on his face. He cups my cheek, his thumb brushing gently against my bottom lip.

"You're always such a good girl for Santa," he murmurs, his voice soft.

I feel a warmth spread through me at his words, a sense of satisfaction and contentment. I've pleased him, and that knowledge fills me with a strange sense of pride.

Michael pulls out of me, and I collapse onto the floor, my body spent. I can feel their cum leaking out of me, and I know I must look like a mess, but I don't care. I feel alive, exhilarated. I feel like a fucking goddess.

Santa begins to dress, his movements slow and deliberate. I watch him, my eyes heavy-lidded with satisfaction. I could watch him all day — his muscular body, his confident movements, the way he fills out that ridiculous padded suit.

As he pulls on his boots, he turns to me, a mischievous glint in his eyes. "You know, every year you seem to get better and better at taking my cock."

I give a low, throaty laugh. "Practice makes perfect, I guess."

"Indeed, it does." His eyes twinkle. "And what a perfect little present you are."

He leans down, pressing a soft kiss to my forehead. "Until next year, baby girl. Be good — but not too good."

With a final chuckle, he climbs back into the chimney, leaving Michael and me alone, wrapped in the afterglow of our unconventional Christmas tradition. Michael helps me off the floor, and we snuggle on the couch.

"Happy Birthday, babe," Michael whispers, pulling me close. "I think this might have been your best one yet."

I nod, my cheek against his chest. "Definitely one for the books."

As we settle in for a well-deserved rest, the Christmas tree lights twinkle in the background, I wonder what next year's visit is going to bring. This is the best birthday and Christmas present every year, and I hope Santa keeps coming to visit. This is my wonderful life — a husband who likes to share me with Santa, and once a year I get to be the sluttiest version of myself.

Best. Life. Ever.

My daughter's laugh pulls me out of my daydream.

"Yeah, mom, as if."

I was telling her parts of the story as I remembered them, leaving most of it out. She heard enough to read between the lines.

She decorates another cookie. "So does dad know you're a slut and lost your virginity to Santa?"

I pick up my frosting-covered knife, and a memory of another Christmas with Santa and frosting makes me smile.

I'm purposely evasive when I answer. "Your dad knows everything about me. We got married Freshman year since I got pregnant the first time he and I had sex."

"Ewww, not that story again. I get it. I use protection."

She takes a bite out of the cookie she just frosted and sighs. "I'd still like to know what relative passed on the gene that made all of us go white haired so young. I'd like to know who to blame."

Michael and I have four kids, and all of them started going white haired as teenagers. Our oldest son, Damien, already has a full head of white hair, and people tease him that he can dress up as Santa someday.

"Maybe I should tell dad that Santa knocked you up, and that's why we have white hair."

I give her a secretive smile. "Maybe you should."

Somehow, I don't think that conversation is going to go the way she thinks it will.

I hold up a cookie in the vague shape of Santa and take a bite of its head and chew. As the sweetness coats my tongue, I think of Santa filling my mouth with his creamy goodness while my husband pounds into my pussy.

Yeah...that conversation would definitely not go the way she expects.

The End

About Lacey Cross

Lacey Cross is a wife-sharing erotica writer with over 100 short stories published since she started in 2021. Her stories emphasize the pleasure found from the wife living her best slut life and embracing the hotwife lifestyle. She explores themes of free use, submissive wives with dominant bulls, BDSM... and oh-so-many men.

Find her books, erotic shorts, and audiobooks on her website:

https://lacey-cross.com/

If you like romantic BDSM erotica, check out her April Cross books at:

https://april-cross.com/